The Little Dandelion Seed THAT HUNG ON

KARYN GWIN

Archway Publishing books may be ordered through booksellers or by contacting:

Archway Publishing
1663 Liberty Drive
Bloomington, IN 47403
www.archwaypublishing.com
844-669-3957

ISBN: 978-1-6657-4938-1 (sc)
ISBN: 978-1-6657-4940-4 (hc)
ISBN: 978-1-6657-4939-8 (e)

Library of Congress Control Number: 2023916245

Print information available on the last page.

Archway Publishing rev. date: 09/06/2023

ARCHWAY PUBLISHING

The Little Dandelion Seed That Hung On

By Karyn Gwin

As the sun reaches high at the top of the sky, a girl walks home from the park with her puppy and her grandma.

As they walk and talk through the light green grass, they pass two young boys surrounded by little flowers. Each boy picks a dandelion puff. They count to three, make a wish and blow the fuzzy little seeds into the air.

4

One of those fuzzy seeds lands on the girl's sleeve. Would you believe that fuzzy little seed hung on?

6

A gentle wind blows and dances with the crows. It swirls and twirls around the girl, but the fuzzy little seed hung on.

8

The grandma spies little bird eyes peeking from a nest. They observe a mama bird hoisting in haste a worm against her chest. As the bird swoops past the girl the little fuzzy seed hung on.

They stop to rest on an old wooden bench under a beautiful flowery tree. They share a big hug beside a ladybug, and the fuzzy little seed hung on.

They see a mama duck with six fluffy babies standing in a row. The curious puppy tries to play with them, but his leash twists around and around the girl like a vine. The little fuzzy seed hung on.

14

They walk past a bush with pretty pink flowers. Suddenly, a wave of beautiful butterflies flutter by. One lands on the girl's nose making her giggle and wiggle. Even then, the fuzzy little seed hung on.

16

During the stroll home a misty spring shower fell from the cottony blue sky. Still, that fuzzy little seed hung on.

As they walk up to the house the little fuzzy seed finally lets go. It catches a ride on a cool glistening raindrop as it falls to the ground.

The rain falls for days till the clouds part ways to let the radiant sun shine. The girl goes outside to play with her puppy. Can you guess what she saw growing in the yard?

One happy little yellow dandelion smiles back at her from the middle of the yard.

THE END